Tillie & Clementine: Zoo Switcheroo

Published by
Happy Fun Books
St. Louis, MO

Please visit
HappyFunBooks.com

ISBN 978-0-9898474-2-1

Printed in Canada

for
Tillie &
Clementine

There once was a girl named Tillie, and she had a sister named Clementine, and they loved to have fun.

One Saturday morning, the girls were lazing in front of the television when Daddy limped home from a jog.

"What's with all this lying about on a beautiful Saturday?" he insisted.
"We need to get you girls out of the house and go have some fun!"

Soon the family was boarding their microbus, but the girls were being stubborn.

Daddy wasn't kidding around. As they pulled into the crowded parking lot, Tillie and Clementine saw the big stone letters and knew they were going to have fun.

They hiked into the zoo with Clementine seated in the kid carrier. Mommy said to her, "Clementine! Aren't you a special girl, getting to ride piggyback on Daddy! How's the view from up there?"

Clementine answered, "Daddy's neck is hairy."

ZEBRAS

SEA LIONS

BIG CATS   BEARS

ELEPHANTS

BUGS   PENGUINS

YAKS   APES

Welcome Desk   Welcome Desk   Welcome Desk

SAFARI GIFTS

KEEP OUR ZOO CLEAN

"I want a snack!" declared Clementine. "Can I have cotton candy?"

"No, you may not," Mommy told her. "We brought our lunch. Let's just watch the bears sleeping."

SNACK SHACK

BEARS

BEARS
URSUS SNOOZUS

"I want a stuffed animal!" announced Clementine. "Let's buy me a stuffed animal!"

"No, Clementine," Daddy replied. "You have plenty of stuffed animals at home. Let's just watch the real animals."

"I want a ride on the train!" yelled Clementine.

"No, that costs extra money," Daddy responded. "You're already getting a ride courtesy of me."

9

At that same zoo there lived a gorilla named Phil, and he had a daughter named LuLu, and they loved to have fun.

While the other gorillas lay around and napped, Phil would look out at all the people with their kids having fun. He wanted very much to take his daughter out there and have fun too.

12

One morning, zookeeper Todd was serving breakfast to the group of gorillas. Phil noticed that he had left the door open.

While Todd wasn't looking, Phil and LuLu slipped out to go have some fun.

But Phil soon realized people were shocked to see him. He didn't understand what the big deal was. After all, he just wanted to take his daughter around the zoo like everyone else.

SNOW CONES

SNOW CONES

14

So they retreated to a hidden corner of the zoo. There Phil sat, trying to think of a way LuLu and he could walk around and have fun without causing a big scene.

Just then, he heard a particularly noisy human family on the other side of the fence. Phil peeked around to see what all the fuss was about.

As the young sisters kept shouting at each other, Phil borrowed some clothes from the noisy family.

On the other side of the fence, Phil and LuLu put on the borrowed clothes. It was kind of fun dressing up like people.

After Clementine threw her stuff away, she noticed something interesting on the ground. LuLu noticed something else interesting, while Phil was focused on adjusting the hat so it would fit better.

As Daddy was checking the ballgame on his phone, he was unaware that the wrong passenger had climbed into the kid carrier.

As Phil was checking his hat, he was unaware that
he was hoisting the wrong rider onto his back.

Daddy marched out into the crowd, trying to catch up with Mommy and Tillie. LuLu was having fun riding in the kid carrier on her dad's back. At least she thought it was her dad, since he had the same hairy neck and arms.

Phil trotted out into the crowd, pleased that his disguise seemed to be working. Clementine was having fun riding horseback on Daddy. At least she thought it was her dad, since he had the same hat, jacket, and hairy neck.

Todd sprinted out into the crowd after he realized he was missing two gorillas. He had just begun his job last week and didn't want to get fired.

While visiting the elephants, Phil reached into his pocket and found a small leather pouch. He wondered if the little green papers inside might come in handy.

And they did! Phil traded some of the green papers for cotton candy. Clementine was glad to finally be getting a good snack.

He traded more green papers for a balloon and stuffed animal. Clementine was really having fun now.

29

And he traded even more green papers for a ride on the Zoo Choo Choo. As the train chugged by, zookeeper Todd caught a glimpse of Phil and saw he had on a red hat and jacket.

30

Todd kept his eyes open for a gorilla in disguise
and anything else out of the ordinary.

31

Later on, Tillie spotted a little girl who looked just like her sister, Clementine. The girl was riding piggyback on a big man who walked sort of funny. He wore clothes like Daddy's, except for his furry pants.

As Tillie got a better look, she saw that it indeed was Clementine on the man's back. She also saw that the man wasn't a man at all, but a gorilla! Tillie tried to point this out to Mommy but couldn't say anything because of her punishment.

Tillie! It's not polite to stand there and stare at people. Come on, we've got to find Daddy and Clementine.

As they caught up with Daddy, Tillie wondered just who this kid was riding on Daddy's back. She noticed the kid was wearing furry pants and a sweater.

Hey, I think I left my hat and jacket by the picnic tables.

That's not like you to misplace things.

It had been a fun day, but Phil decided it was time for LuLu and him to go home. On the way back, he stopped to return the clothes where he first found them.

As the two dads set down the two piggyback-riding daughters, LuLu and Clementine heard familiar voices on the opposite sides of the fence.

Clementine and LuLu went to investigate and came face to face with each other.

38

They turned back to say something to their dads, and that's when each realized she had been riding piggyback on the wrong dad.

LuLu smiled at Clementine
and gave her the hat.

Clementine smiled at LuLu
and gave her the balloon.

Clementine ran up to Tillie, and they gave each other a great big hug.

"I can't find my hat or jacket," said Daddy, "but I did find two young sisters who like each other again."

LuLu jumped up and gave her dad a great big hug too. Phil was glad she appreciated spending the day with him exploring the zoo.

The father and daughter gorillas hustled back to the ape house, this time careful not to be seen by all the zoo visitors.

It had been a fun day, and now the family walked back to their microbus. The girls skipped ahead as Mommy and Daddy chatted.

P-U, honey! Your jacket stinks.

Yeah, and it's all stretched out too - like some big beast was walking around in it.

44

Todd threw his net over the smelly, hairy figure in the red hat and jacket. He thought he had finally caught his escaped gorillas. Mommy explained that Daddy was not a gorilla, and after Daddy showed his driver's license he was free to go.

That night, Tillie and Clementine told their parents a tale about an incredible mix-up at the zoo.

Mommy laughed at the girls' imagination, but as he looked in his empty wallet, Daddy wondered if this zoo switcheroo was really true.

The End